I Don't Like Birthday Parties

WELBECK

Lucas was a boy who did
not like birthday parties.

He couldn't really explain it,
but something about birthday
parties made his insides go all

squooshy, gooshy

and his brain feel

squiggly, wiggly.

Every party was the same.

Loud! Crowded. Chaotic.

He would watch
the others having fun,
but never joined in.

More than anything, Lucas wanted to enjoy
birthday parties like everyone else.

So, when he received an invitation to another party,
Lucas made a decision.

If he wanted to like birthday parties, he would have
to *act* like someone who *liked* birthday parties.

"I will be braver than ever before!"
he thought, as he drew out a plan.

When he arrived at the party the next week, his belly felt like he had swallowed a **billion** butterflies.

It was just like all
the other parties.

Loud.
Crowded.
Chaotic.

"Do you want a tattoo?" a girl called out to him.
He didn't, but remembering his plan, Lucas nodded.

He picked the smallest tattoo he could find.

It felt **slimy** and **sticky** on his hand.
He rubbed it off when no one was looking.

Lucas tried the bouncy castle.

The **wobbly, wiggly** floor

made it hard to balance.

He got **bumped** right
and **banged** left.

He fell down and struggled to
get back up again, then quickly
bounced out.

Lucas *even* played the party games,
but the other kids were too fast for him.

He was being braver
than ever before,
but he wasn't having fun.

When all the children gathered together for a photo, Lucas stood on the very end.

He didn't feel happy.

The bright **flashes** from the cameras hurt his eyes and he didn't like everyone looking at him.

Just then, some very loud music
started playing and a group
of children ran past him.

Lucas stopped. His head felt **dizzy** and his legs felt like **jelly**.
Everything was getting noisier and busier, until...

...POP!

A big balloon burst behind him. It was all too much. He had tried, but his plan had failed.

Lucas felt like being alone,
so he crawled under the closest table.

Unfortunately, Kate from his class was already there.
Then, the singing started. Lucas sighed.
"I don't like that song either," whispered Kate.

After the singing, Kate left for
a moment, but soon returned
with two pieces of delicious
double-chocolate cake.

"Cake is the only good part about parties,"
Lucas said, with a grateful smile.

"I never have people sing to me on my birthday," Kate replied. "Last year, I invited two friends. We made sundaes with whipped cream and sprinkles!"

Lucas liked the sound of that.

"You didn't have a big party?" Lucas asked, quietly.
"No music? No games? No singing?"

"No, no and NO WAY!"

"I don't like birthday parties," replied Lucas, "but that sounds like fun!"

That night, Lucas crossed out his
old plan and got to work on a
new idea for his birthday.

And on his birthday, everything went exactly as planned.

Lucas realised he *wasn't* a boy who didn't like
birthday parties ...

... he just enjoyed them in his own special way.

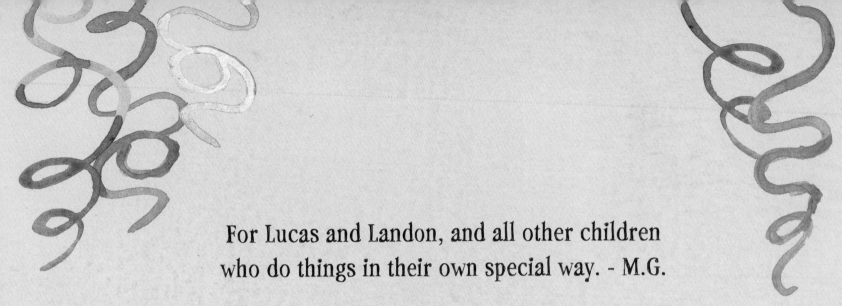

For Lucas and Landon, and all other children
who do things in their own special way. - M.G.

Maureen Gaspari is the creator of the website, *www.thehighlysensitivechild.com*.
This site provides parenting support for those raising highly sensitive children with sensory challenges
and anxiety and aims to promote understanding, acceptance and appreciation.

To my generous and clever parents, for always making sure
we had access to books, paper, pencils and paint. - S.K.

Children with high sensitivity or neurodevelopmental challenges often experience
sensory overload, which means they find loud noises, busy places and too many
people overwhelming. It can be very stressful for the children, causing them to feel
excluded, and anxious about new places or events. This wonderful book addresses
these issues in a helpful and positive way by telling the story of Lucas, who doesn't
like birthday parties, but discovers a way to celebrate that makes him feel comfortable
and secure. The story helps children and their parents make sense of overwhelming
feelings and overstimulation, by normalising such experiences and
acknowledging that different needs are always valid.

Lauren Callaghan
Consultant Clinical Psychologist